The Warrior and the Wise Man

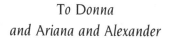

To Donna
and Ariana and Alexander

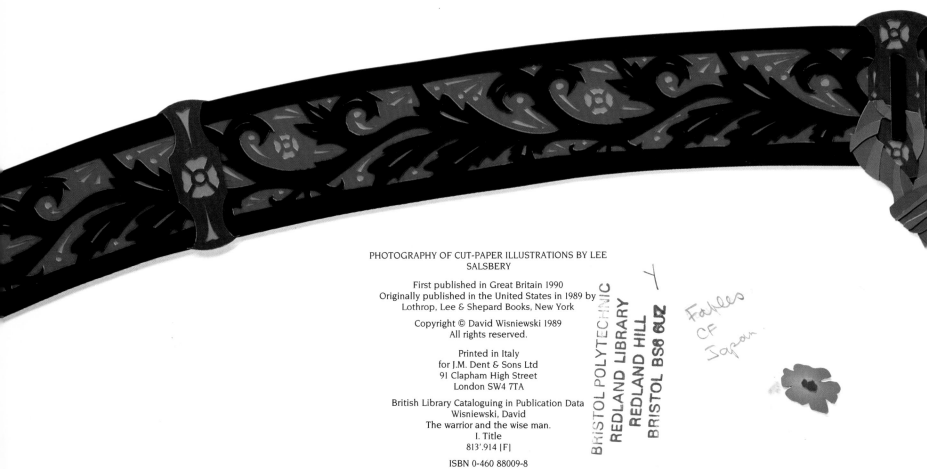

PHOTOGRAPHY OF CUT-PAPER ILLUSTRATIONS BY LEE
SALSBERY

First published in Great Britain 1990
Originally published in the United States in 1989 by
Lothrop, Lee & Shepard Books, New York

Printed in Italy
for J.M. Dent & Sons Ltd
91 Clapham High Street
London SW4 7TA

British Library Cataloguing in Publication Data
Wisniewski, David
The warrior and the wise man.
I. Title
813'.914 [F]

ISBN 0-460 88009-8

The Warrior and the Wise Man

STORY AND PICTURES BY DAVID WISNIEWSKI

J.M. Dent & Sons Ltd
London

Long Ago In Japan, An Emperor Had Twin Sons. They Were Alike In every feature and gesture, yet very different in nature and temperament.

Tozaemon, brave and fierce, was the greatest warrior in the land.

Toemon, thoughtful and gentle, was the greatest wise man in the land.

One day the emperor called his sons to him. "Someday one of you shall sit upon this throne," he said, "yet to decide between two such excellent sons is impossible. Therefore, I propose a trial.

"The world is made of five eternal elements: the Earth That Is Ever Bountiful, the Water That Constantly Quenches, the Fire That Burns Forever, the Wind That Always Blows, and the Cloud That Eternally Covers. Each is guarded by a monstrous demon and his army.

"The first to bring me these five things shall rule."

In the morning, the brothers set out.

Tozaemon was first to arrive at the garden of the Earth Demon. Great trees and beautiful flowers sprang up before his eyes, but Tozaemon ignored them. "I am Tozaemon!" he cried to the soldiers at the gate. "I demand a portion of the Earth That Is Ever Bountiful!"

The soldiers tried to block his way, but Tozaemon spurred his horse forward into the garden, crushing flowers and snapping branches. He scooped up a handful of earth and galloped off, with the Earth Demon's army close behind.

When Toemon arrived, the Earth Demon stopped tending the broken trees to glare at him. "If I find the man who did this," he rumbled, "I shall grind him to powder to flavour my tea."

"A thousand apologies for the actions of my brother," Toemon replied. "May I offer my humble service in repairing what he damaged?"

The Earth Demon accepted Toemon's help in the garden. At day's end, he gave Toemon a box of the Earth That Is Ever Bountiful. They bowed graciously to each other and Toemon continued on his way.

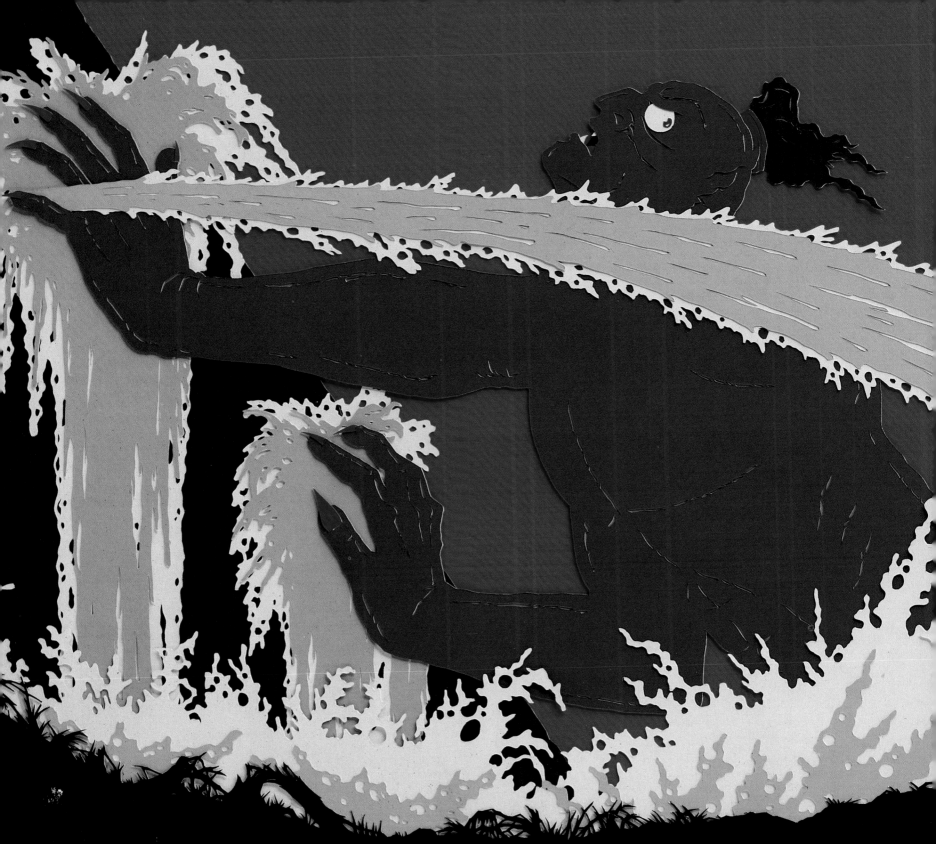

As Toemon approached the well of the Water Demon, he saw that once again his twin had been before him. The Water Demon was repairing a hundred holes in the stony sides of his well. The water gushing out had flooded the demon's kingdom.

"My lord!" shouted Toemon. "I have with me a portion of the Earth That Is Ever Bountiful. As my brother is responsible for your distress, may I offer it for the renewal of your lands?"

The demon took the box and scattered its contents on the sodden ground. Immediately mighty trees, fresh flowers, and new grass sprang from the soil.

The grateful demon handed Toemon a sealed jar. "The Water That Constantly Quenches," he said, and bowed.

Toemon was urging his donkey toward the cave of the Fire Demon when his brother raced by with the army of the Fire Demon on his heels. Inside the cave, the Fire Demon stood waist-deep in glowing lava, striving to replace the broken door of his giant furnace. When he spied Toemon, he roared, "You dare to return?"

"No, my lord," Toemon replied. "It is my twin brother who has created this difficulty."

"I thirst!" the Fire Demon cried. "If I had but a little water to soothe my burning tongue, I could complete this task!"

"Here is the Water That Constantly Quenches!" Toemon shouted. He tossed the sealed jar to the Fire Demon, who downed the contents in a single gulp. Then with one mighty heave the demon snapped the door back into place. He fashioned a bowl of lava and filled it with flame.

"In return for the drink," said the demon, handing the bowl to Toemon, "here is the Fire That Burns Forever."

As Toemon neared the castle of the Wind Demon, a single horseman burst through the gates and galloped toward him. In his mailed fist Tozaemon clutched a delicate fan. Behind him, the Wind Demon's army was boiling out of the ruined gates.

Toemon entered the castle to find the Wind Demon sitting in the gale-whipped great hall. A huge torch smoked uselessly in his hand. "I need light!" the demon boomed. "If I had seen him, I could have caught him!"

"My lord!" Toemon called. "Perhaps the Fire That Burns Forever will satisfy your appetite for my brother!" He lit the demon's torch, which burned steadily despite the great wind.

The Wind Demon gave Toemon a small fan, like the one he had seen in Tozaemon's hand. "One flutter," said the demon, "will start the Wind That Always Blows."

When he reached the mountain of the Cloud Demon, Toemon saw a man descend from the misty peak, mount a horse, and gallop away, a grey-clad army in pursuit.

At the top of the cloud-wrapped mountain, Toemon could not tell ground from sky in the thick haze. "Hello!" he called.

"Hello!" a voice called back.

"Where are you?" Toemon cried.

"Where are *you*?"

"Here!" shouted Toemon. He waved the fan, and a gust of wind parted the mist. There stood the Cloud Demon, swords raised.

"Marvellous!" cried the demon. "To see things clearly again!" But already the mists were stealing back.

"Do not despair, my lord," Toemon said. "As my brother has occasioned such an uproar, you may certainly have the Wind That Always Blows."

The demon caught a fine white cloud and corked it in a flask. "And for you," he said, "the Cloud That Eternally Covers."

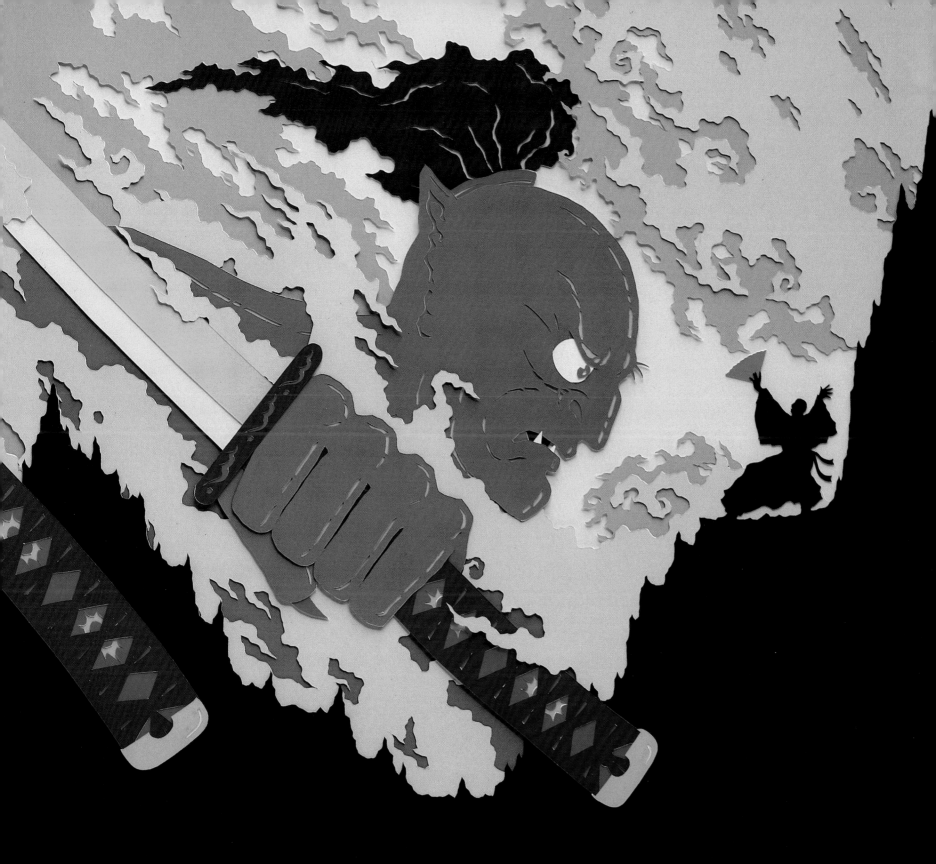

Toemon was still far from his father's castle when the sounds of celebration reached his ears. He made his way to the pavilion where the emperor was greeting the triumphant Tozaemon.

Suddenly a terrible wail rose from the battlements: "We are lost!"

The emperor and his court ran to see what was amiss. Toemon and Tozaemon ran with them.

There, as far as the eye could see, stood the combined armies of the five demons. As one, they lifted their voices in a hideous shout: "Give us Tozaemon!"

Tozaemon turned to his father. "Though I have won your kingdom," he said sadly, "in so doing, I have lost my life."

Then he turned to Toemon. "My compliments, brother," he said. "The throne will be yours." He drew his sword and prepared to descend to the gates.

"Wait!" shouted Toemon. He uncorked the flask, and the Cloud That Eternally Covers billowed into the air, shielding the castle from view. "Give me the other elements you took," he begged his brother. Puzzled, Tozaemon gave them to him.

Toemon opened the box of Earth That Is Ever Bountiful and sprinkled it on the ground below. Instantly a bulwark of enormous trees sprang up, blocking the armies' advance.

Then Toemon released the Fire That Burns Forever. A towering wall of flame roared toward the armies. The soldiers broke ranks and fled.

Toemon poured out the Water That Constantly Quenches. The thundering wave extinguished the fire and carried the fleeing armies before it, depositing them wet, shivering, and defeated

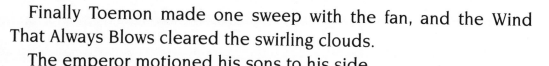

Finally Toemon made one sweep with the fan, and the Wind That Always Blows cleared the swirling clouds.

The emperor motioned his sons to his side.

"Today I have learned a great truth," he proclaimed. "Strength, though vital, must always be in the service of wisdom. For that reason, Toemon will become the next emperor of this land."

And so he did, and no emperor before or since has ruled as well as he.

AUTHOR'S NOTE

When I had the idea for a story that would dramatize the contrast between two approaches to solving a problem, one relying on blind force and the other on reasoned action, I chose to set it in ancient Japan, a society that had clearly defined classes of warriors and wise men.

In the twelfth century, when Japan was torn by civil war, a class of warriors arose. Known as *samurai*, meaning "one who serves," they were completely dedicated to *bushido*, "the way of the warrior." As the emperor's son, Tozaemon would not have been of the samurai class, but he would have received martial training. The samurai's crested helmet with armoured neck guard, lightweight flexible armour of silk-laced metal strips, and two razor-sharp swords are reproduced in Tozaemon's silhouette.

At the same time, this society respected the way of the wise. From earliest times Japan has nourished a deep regard for beauty and tranquility, especially as evidenced in the natural world. The five universal elements of earth, water, fire, wind, and cloud that are the object of the twins' quest in the story were celebrated in Shinto, Japan's native religion. When Buddhism reached Japan in the sixth century, it partook of Shinto's calm appreciation of natural beauty.

Among the sects of Buddhism that flourished at the time of the samurai was Zen, whose adherents practised meditation in the hope of gaining enlightenment. The life of a Zen monk was simple and austere, though rigorous both physically and mentally. While the emperor's son would not have been a monk, Toemon's shaved head, plain robe, and bamboo walking stick identify him as one who has received Zen training. The way he deals with obstacles indicates that he was trained in the early period of Zen, when the teachings emphasized the importance of logic. Also drawn from Buddhism are the five demons, which are based on statues of guardian deities found outside Buddhist temples.

Many details in the illustrations are derived from my research into Japanese decorative arts. Patterns such as the flowered wainscotting behind the emperor and the grillwork of the wind demon's palace are taken from textile designs. The emperor's *shotoku* robe and head dress were copied from a twelfth-century costume that actually was black, as seen here. The display of flowers behind the emperor is modelled on a traditional *ikebana* arrangement. The large flower between two small ones, seen on the emperor's fan and ornamenting the pavilion and palace, is a symbol adopted by a noble twelfth-century family; these symbols, called *mon*, were often floral designs. I chose this one because it so beautifully represented the emperor and his two sons.

In a few instances I have allowed myself artistic licence in adapting authentic details to the needs of the book. The sword on the title page combines the ornate scabbard of a twelfth-century weapon with the silk-cord hilt wrapping and leather (or ray skin) strap mounting that would have been used four hundred years later. The earlier sword would have had an equally elaborate matching hilt and a mounting of woven metal chain to attach it to the wearer's belt, impossible to render in cut paper. A warrior probably would not have brought his weapons into the emperor's presence, but Tozaemon wears his swords here so that his identity and character are immediately apparent to the reader.

When the story and sketches were taking shape, I needed names for my characters. I asked Mr Yamada of the Japanese Information Centre in Washington, D.C., if he could suggest names for twins that would incorporate a set of opposites. He kindly suggested Tozaemon (pronounced TOE-ZAY-MON) and Toemon (TOE-AY-MON). The Japanese calligraphy for these names is identical except for the second character, which in Tozaemon means "left" and in Toemon means "right." When I looked over my sketches, I was amazed to discover that Tozaemon always appeared on the left and Toemon on the right.

The illustrations are cut from Chrome-arama art papers and adhered with double-stick photo mountings. Each figure's silhouette is transferred to the back of a sheet of black paper. The outline is inked with a technical pen and then cut out with an X-Acto knife. Coloured papers are cut in the same way for backgrounds, buildings, and decorations. More than eight hundred blades were used to produce the illustrations for this book.